Are We Having Fun Yet?

by Susie Ngyuen • illustrated by Brad Teare

Harcourt

Orlando   Boston   Dallas   Chicago   San Diego

Visit *The Learning Site!*

www.harcourtschool.com

"We're going to have a lot of fun on this trip," said Papá.

"We will if we ever get in the car," Mama said.

Mama, Papá, Grandma, Grandpa, and I were going to Florida. We were going to visit my aunt, uncle, and cousin. They have a house near the beach. I was excited about our trip. I knew that Florida was going to be fun.

Grandma asked me, "Ana, what are you doing with all those stuffed animals?"

"I'm taking them to Florida," I said.

Mama put her arm around me and said, "That's not a good idea, *niña*. We don't have room. Why not take just one?"

"Pick a small one," said Papá.

I was unhappy. "The animals will be sad," I said.

Mama said, "With all your animals in the car, there won't be room for Grandpa. Then he will be sad."

So only my stuffed bunny went to Florida. Maybe the animals that stayed home were lucky, because the trip didn't go exactly as we planned.

It took us a long time to get to Florida. We got lost three times. Papá said that Mama read the map wrong. Mama said that Papá should stop and ask for directions.

Then we had a flat tire. We had to unload the car, and Papá and Grandpa tried to change the tire. By the time the tire was fixed, we were hungry, tired, and dusty. We repacked the car quickly. This was already a long trip!

When we got to Florida, Aunt Maya, Uncle Emilio, and my cousin Ernesto came out of the house to welcome us.

"My stomach hurts. I'm tired of sitting in this car," said Grandma. She opened the door and got out as fast as she could.

"At least your clothes aren't covered with dirt like mine are," Grandpa said.

"What a long trip!" Mama said as she hugged her sister, Aunt Maya.

"We're so glad to see you!" Aunt Maya said. "How was your trip?"

We all just groaned.

"It's so hot!" I complained.

"It's perfect for swimming," said Uncle Emilio.

My aunt and uncle helped Mama and Papá carry all our things in the house. Ernesto helped me carry my bag inside.

"Do you want to go to the beach?" asked Ernesto.

I could feel the sweat on my upper lip. "Yes," I said. "I need to cool off!"

I looked out the window. People walking by had red faces. I wondered if this trip was going to be fun, after all. Maybe going to Florida hadn't been such a good idea.

Then I saw a cute little dog sitting on the sidewalk. He looked hot, too.

"Whose dog is that?" I asked.

Ernesto said, "I don't know. He was there yesterday, too. He must be lost."

"Let's give him some food," I said.

We got some leftover hamburgers from the kitchen.

"What is that for?" asked Uncle Emilio.

Ernesto said, "We're feeding a lost dog."

"Was this your idea, Ana?" asked Mama. "If you feed that dog now, he'll come back tomorrow for more."

"I'll just feed him once," I said.

"This is a mistake," said my Grandpa.

Papá said, "Ana, you may feed that dog
tonight, but we are not taking it home with us."

Ernesto and I went out and fed the dog. He
wagged his tail and licked our hands.

We went back inside. Ernesto said, "That dog
is really cute!"

The dog looked at the house and barked.

"Can he come in?" I begged. "He looks hot."

"What should we name him?" Ernesto asked.

Papá said, "He's not our dog! He won't be our dog! Don't give him a name!"

I whispered to Ernesto, "His name is Sammy."

The next morning, I put on shorts and a t-shirt. I put on plenty of sunscreen, too. I was trying to stay cool.

Papá asked, "Who wants to play tennis with me?"

No one spoke. Then I said, "Can't we go swimming instead?"

"That's a good idea," said Papá.

It felt nice on the beach. The wind was blowing, and I could smell the salty air. Papá took his tennis shoes off and tugged at his socks. He said, "I'm going in the water."

He walked into the water and stood there for a few seconds. Then he hurried out of the water.

He hopped around on the sand.

"Is the water cold?" I asked.

"Yes," Papá said. "It feels cold at first. But you'll get used to it. Come on. I'll race you to the water."

We ran toward the waves and splashed in the water. I accidentally swallowed some ocean water. It tasted terrible!

Pretty soon Papá said, "We need to go home. You're getting a sunburn."

I wasn't ready to leave the beach, though. This trip was just starting to be fun!

As we got to the house, I saw the little dog. He saw me and wagged his tail.

"Hi, Sammy!" I cried. I leaned down to pet him.

"You know, he is a cute dog," said Papá.

When we went inside, my mother said, "I saw you petting that dog, Ana. Remember, we are not keeping him."

That afternoon, a nice breeze was blowing and it was a little cooler. Grandpa said that he wanted to take a boat ride.

We were a few miles from the shore when the waves started to get higher and higher. Water splashed everywhere, and everyone got very wet. Ernesto got a stomachache. He had to go to bed early that night.

The water ruined my favorite pair of shoes. And Papá was right. I had a sunburn. It was painful!

Later that day, I saw Papá and my uncle in front of the house. They were playing with Sammy. Papá gave Sammy a piece of bread and patted his head. He brought Sammy inside with him.

When he saw me, he said, "He's a nice dog, but we're still not taking him home."

I could tell that he was beginning to like the dog. I said, "His name is Sammy."

I hoped that Papá would change his mind.

The next morning I was still sore from my sunburn. Sammy was standing at the foot of my bed. He had Papá's slippers in his mouth! He had chewed right through one of them. Papá was going to be angry.

"Oh, Sammy. Now Papá will never let me take you home," I cried.

I told Mama about Papá's slippers, and she said it was all right.

Uncle Emilio and Aunt Maya took Ernesto and me to a carnival. We ate and ate. We rode a merry-go-round and a roller coaster.

Ernesto got sick again. I didn't feel well either.

When we got back to the house, Mama was sitting with Sammy in her lap. She smiled and said, "You know, he is a friendly little dog."

By the end of the week, I was ready to go home. I wanted the trip to end. But I didn't want to leave Sammy.

Mama, Papá, Grandma, Grandpa, and I got in the car. Sammy was looking at us. He looked sad. Papá closed the door and started the car. But then he got out and opened the door to the back seat.

"Here, Sammy," he said. Sammy jumped into the car, and off we drove.

So Sammy did come home with us after all. Sammy is our dog now. I guess it was a great trip, after all.